DISNEY · PIXAR
THE WORLD OF
Cars

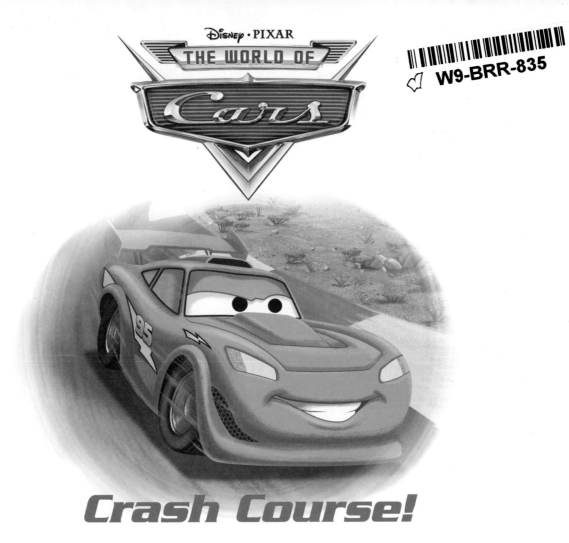

Crash Course!

By Frank Berrios
Based on a story by Annie Auerbach
Illustrated by the Disney Storybook Artists

Random House 🏠 New York

Library of Congress Control Number: 2009929441   ISBN: 978-0-7364-2650-3   www.randomhouse.com/kids
MANUFACTURED IN CHINA   10

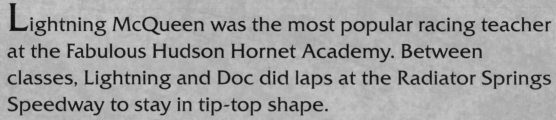

Lightning McQueen was the most popular racing teacher at the Fabulous Hudson Hornet Academy. Between classes, Lightning and Doc did laps at the Radiator Springs Speedway to stay in tip-top shape.

"All right, kid, let's see if you can set a new record," said Doc Hudson.

"Sure—watch this!" replied Lightning as he zoomed ahead.

Meanwhile, students at the Chick Hicks Racing Academy learned Chick's golden rules of racing, the three Cs: cheat, cheat, and cheat! Chick's favorite student was a sleek, steel-gray racer named Switcher.

Chick taught Switcher all of his best dirty tricks.

When a two-car race was announced
as part of the Race-O-Rama series, Chick Hicks
wanted to make sure he'd win. He trained Switcher every day to
guarantee that his racing partner was in prime shape.

"You call that speed?" Chick called out. "Grandma Hicks can
drive faster than you!"

Switcher narrowed his eyes and sped up to 150 miles per hour!
Chick nodded. "That's more like it."

When race day arrived, excitement filled the air. The stands were packed bumper to bumper with screaming fans.

"*That's* our competition?" said Switcher loudly, looking over at Lightning and Mater. "I could beat them with my eyes closed."

"Oh, you'll have your eyes closed—because you'll be crying when we win!" Lightning shot back. *"Ka-chow!"*

Before Switcher could reply, the green flag
dropped—and the race was on!

Lightning took the lead, but Switcher and Chick
were right behind him, followed by Mater.

"Get out of my way!" Chick growled at Lightning.

"Gladly," replied Lightning as he poured on the
speed and left Chick in the dust.

Switcher shifted gears and shot in front of Lightning. Then he released an oil slick! Lightning slid in the oil, but managed to stay on the track.

"Now I'm going to win this race," Switcher boasted to Chick. "See you at the finish line."

Chick didn't like the sound of that.

"If Switcher thinks he's taking first place, he's in for a surprise," Chick said, gaining speed.

BAM! Chick rammed Switcher into the wall!

Switcher flipped over and over until he came to a stop in the infield. "But I'm on *your* team!" the wrecked race car yelled.

"First place is *mine*!" Chick replied.

Unfortunately for Chick, his last dirty trick had cost him the race. Lightning and Mater had already won and were making their way to the podium to receive their Silver Tailfin Trophy.

"Here's to teamwork," said Mater.

"And to friends you can count on," replied Lightning. *"Ka-chow!"*

Lightning easily crossed the finish line first. *"Ka-chow!"* he said, beaming.

Sarge and Lightning smiled as they collected their Silver Tailfin Trophy. They knew that winners never cheat, and cheaters never win.

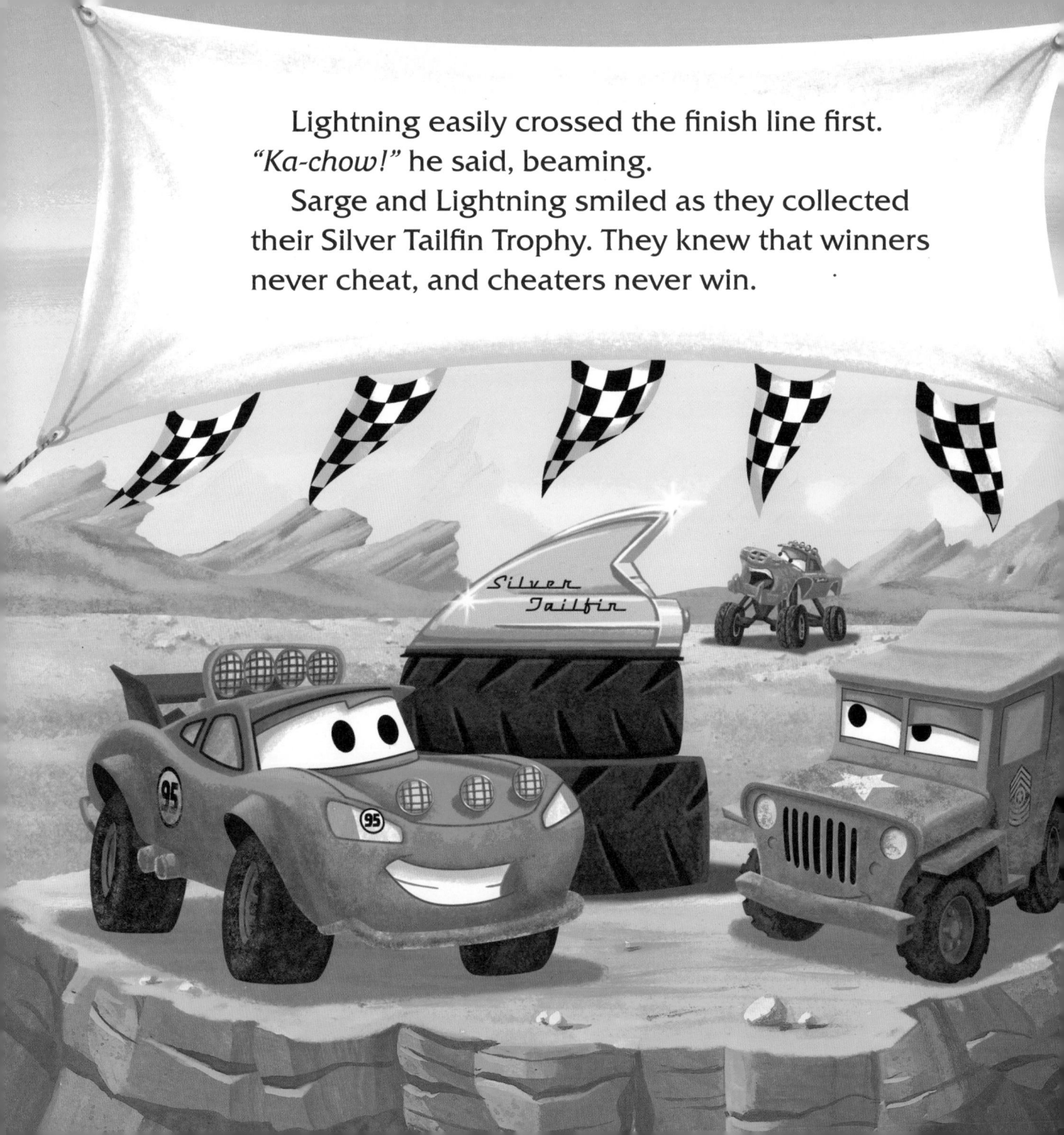

Just before the sand beds, Lightning pulled into the lead. Suddenly, a burst of dusty sand exploded around him!

Lightning couldn't see a thing in the cloudy mess, but he remembered to keep racing forward. He floored the gas and shot out of the sand beds. El Machismo choked on Lightning's trail of dust.

Lightning and El Machismo roared onto the course. They zoomed across the desert plains, took tight corners, jumped hills, and raced over a rickety bridge. Nothing seemed to slow El Machismo down.

"Uh-oh," Lightning said to himself. "This guy is tougher than I thought."

Halfway through the race, Chick sped in front of Sarge and released a bunch of bolts onto the ground—one of his favorite dirty tricks. But Sarge veered off the path and skillfully bounced across the rocky terrain. Chick was so busy looking at Sarge that he ran right into a giant cactus.

Now it was Lightning McQueen and El Machismo's turn to race!

Sarge and Chick pulled up to the starting line.

"Get ready to lose, old man," Chick growled, gunning his motor.

"Get ready to lose to *this* old man," Sarge replied as the green flag dropped.

On race day, the two teams rolled into Autovia. Both Lightning and Chick had been upgraded with fog lights and all-terrain tires.

"Bow down to the tower of power! Oh, yeeeeaaaaah!" roared El Machismo.

The crowd was amazed by the size of the big truck, but Sarge and Lightning weren't scared. They were focused on winning!

Sarge saved his most important off-road racing lesson for last.

"To win this race," said Sarge, "you have to know how to handle one thing: sand. It's impossible to see through, and you'll want to stop. But just keep going."

"Yes, sir!" Lightning replied as Sarge demonstrated his off-road racing skills on an obstacle course.

Training started at dawn the next morning.
"All right, soldier, give me twenty-five miles!
Go!" Sarge barked.
"Ow, ow, ow!" said Lightning
as he raced up a hill.

Since the first event was going to be a relay race, Lightning McQueen needed to find an off-road racing partner. When Sarge stopped by to watch his friends practice, Lightning had an idea.

"Hey, Sarge, why don't *you* race with me?"

"Sounds like a plan, soldier. But first *you* need some training," said Sarge. "When I'm finished with you, you'll find dirt in places you didn't know you had!"

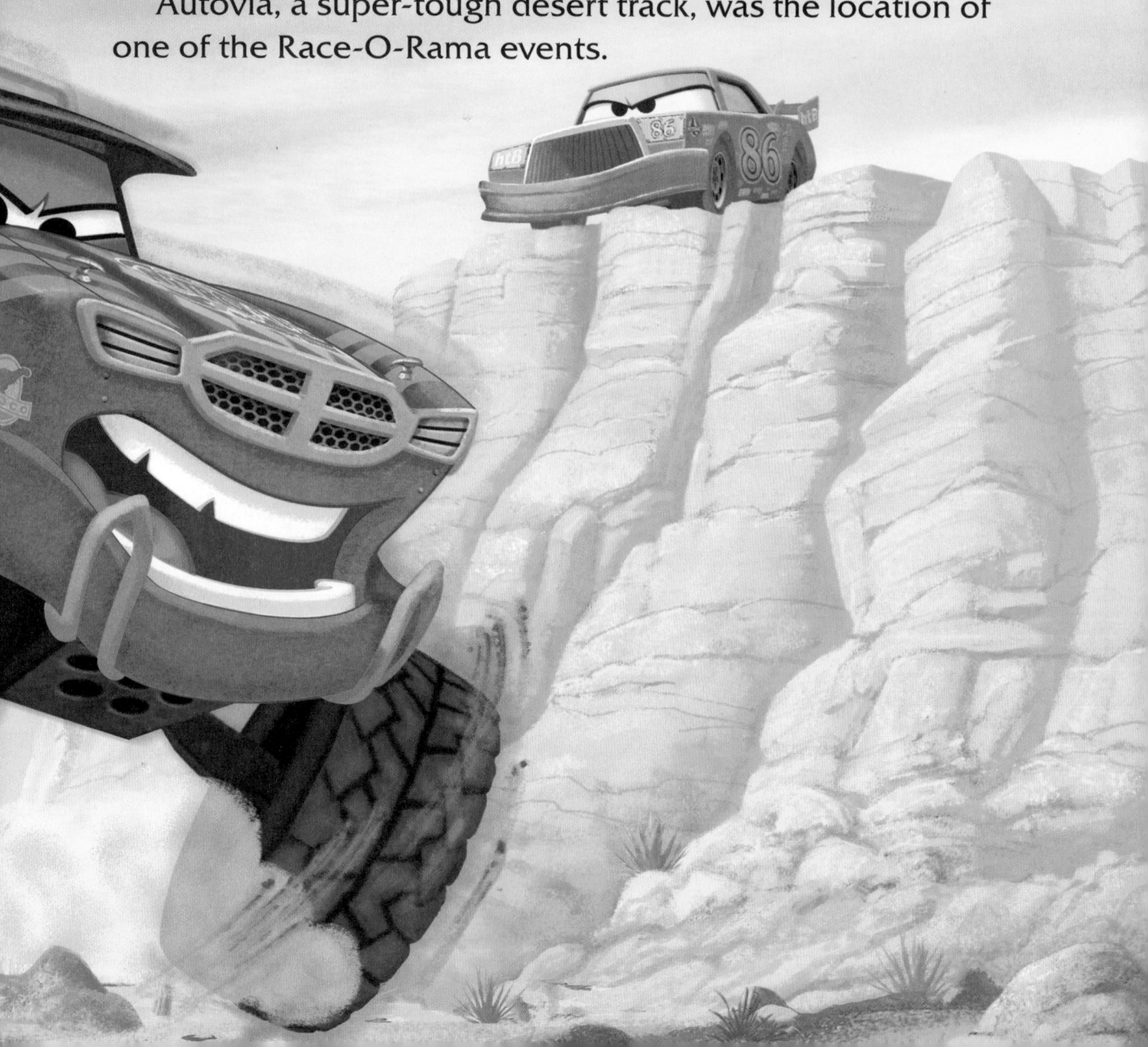

"El Machismo is going to crush Lightning McQueen at Autovia!" Chick said with a sneer.

Autovia, a super-tough desert track, was the location of one of the Race-O-Rama events.

El Machismo raced through the canyon, enjoying every rocky bump and bounce. Driving across rough terrain was what he was built for.

From the cliff above, Chick Hicks watched his prized student.

Off-road Racers!

By Frank Berrios

Based on a story by Annie Auerbach

Illustrated by the Disney Storybook Artists

Random House 🏠 New York